For Grannie and Grandpa

LITTLE TIGER PRESS
An imprint of Magi Publications
1 The Coda Centre, 189 Munster Road
London SW6 6AW
First published in Great Britain 2000
Text and illustrations © 2000 Joanne Partis
Joanne Partis has asserted her rights to be identified
as the author and illustrator of this work under the
Copyright, Designs and Patents Act, 1988.
Printed in Belgium
All rights reserved • ISBN 1 85430 634 0
3 5 7 9 10 8 6 4 2

Joanne Partis

Hungry Harry

LITTLE TIGER PRESS

London

Harry Frog was feeling hungry.
"What's for dinner?" he asked his mum.
"Well, I think you're old enough to look for your own food now," said Mummy Frog.

"Brilliant!" cried Harry, and off
he leaped across the lily pond . . .

till he came to some tall reeds.
"There's sure to be something tasty
here," said Harry, licking his lips.

Sure enough, there
was a delicious-looking
dragonfly. Harry was just
about to jump when . . .

the dragonfly flew off, high
into the air.
"You can't eat me!" she called.
"I'm much too quick for you."

Harry was wondering
what to do next when
suddenly he saw . . .

a big juicy caterpillar
on a twig above him.

"Goody, goody, dinner at last!" cried Harry, but when he flicked out his long tongue to catch it . . .

the caterpillar
laughed. "You can't
eat me!" she said.
"My hairs would
tickle your tongue."

"Never mind, I'll find something soon," said Harry.
He bounced on until he met . . .

a scrumptious-looking snail crawling towards him.

"Yummy, yummy," said Harry, but when he reached it . . .

the snail's head suddenly disappeared!
"You can't eat me!" said the
snail from inside its shell.
"I'm much too clever."

Harry was getting hungrier and hungrier.
He was just about to give up and go
home to his mum, when he spotted . . .

a squirmy worm, wriggling along.
"Now's my chance!" cried Harry, but just as he was about to catch the worm in his big wide mouth . . .

it slithered down into a
wormhole.
"You can't eat me!"
shouted the worm. "I'm
too squiggly and squirmy."

Harry felt very fed up. He would go home to his mum. But just as he turned to hop back, he saw something he'd never seen before . . .

It didn't look too quick . . .

It didn't look too tickly . . .

It didn't look too clever . . .

And it didn't look
too squiggly and
squirmy.

In fact it looked . . .

And, what was more . . .

there was enc

ugh for everyone!